To my dear friends and family,

To my dear friends and cherished family members, whose unwavering support and love have been the threads that bind us together in the fabric of life. Your encouragement and understanding have illuminated my path, guiding me through the complexities of honesty and deceit. This book is dedicated to each one of you, with heartfelt gratitude for your presence in my journey.

With love,

Thangjam Ramananda Singh

THE TAPESTRY OF HONESTY: UNRAVELING DECEIT IN THE FAMILY

THANGJAM RAMANANDA SINGH

Made with ♥ on the Notion Press Platform
www.notionpress.com

Contents

Foreword

In "The Tapestry of Honesty: Unraveling Deceit in the Family," Thangjam Ramananda Singh invites us into a world where the delicate threads of truth and falsehood intersect within the confines of family life. With poignant insight and heartfelt storytelling, Singh navigates the complexities of honesty and deceit, exploring the profound impact they have on familial relationships.

Through the lens of Luther and Melody's journey, Singh sheds light on the universal struggles faced by families grappling with deception. As we embark on this introspective exploration, we are challenged to confront our perceptions of truth and integrity and to consider how they shape our interactions with those we hold dear.

With wisdom and compassion, Singh reminds us that honesty is not merely a virtue but a fundamental cornerstone of genuine connection. As we unravel the intricacies of deceit within the family, may we emerge with a deeper understanding of the power of honesty to mend the fabric of our lives.

Thangjam Ramananda Singh

Preface

In "The Tapestry of Honesty: Unraveling Deceit in the Family," we embark on a profound journey into the heart of familial relationships, where the delicate threads of honesty and deception intersect. Through the lens of Luther and Melody's experiences, we are invited to explore the complexities of truth-telling and the profound impact it has on the fabric of family life.

As we navigate through the pages of this book, we confront uncomfortable truths about the prevalence of deceit within our own families and communities. We are challenged to confront our own biases and assumptions and to consider how our actions shape the narratives of those we love most.

Through introspection and reflection, we are called to unravel the intricate layers of deception that often cloud our perceptions of reality. In doing so, we pave the way for healing and transformation, forging deeper connections built on a foundation of trust and authenticity.

"The Tapestry of Honesty" serves as a guiding light, illuminating the path towards greater understanding and compassion within our families. May this journey inspire us to embrace truth in all its forms and to weave a tapestry of honesty that binds us together in love and understanding.

Thangjam Ramananda Singh

Acknowledgements

I would like to express my heartfelt gratitude to all those who have supported me throughout the journey of conducting this research and writing this book.

First and foremost, I am deeply thankful to my family for their unwavering support, encouragement, and understanding. Their belief in my abilities and constant encouragement kept me motivated during the challenging moments of this endeavor.

A special thanks go to my friends for their encouragement, understanding, and unwavering support throughout this solitary journey of research and writing. Your words of encouragement and belief in my work meant the world to me and kept me going during moments of self-doubt.

Lastly, I extend my sincere appreciation to the readers who will engage with this work. I hope that the research presented in this book will spark curiosity, contribute to knowledge in the field, and inspire others to embark on their journeys of discovery.

To my family, friends, and all those who have supported me along the way, thank you for believing in me and for being a constant source of inspiration.

Warm regards,
Thangjam Ramananda Singh

Prologue

In the quiet suburbs of Thangmeiband Valley, nestled among the rolling hills of Manipur, lies a house that holds the secrets of a family torn apart by deception. Luther and Melody, once the epitome of marital bliss, find themselves embroiled in a web of lies spun by their sons, Roger and Rupesh.

As the story unfolds, we are invited into the inner sanctum of the family home, where tensions simmer beneath the surface and truths long buried begin to resurface. With each passing day, Luther and Melody grapple with the unsettling realization that their sons may not be the honest and trustworthy individuals they once believed them to be.

Against the backdrop of a vibrant and bustling community, where gossip spreads like wildfire and reputations hang in the balance, the family's facade begins to crumble. Dark secrets and hidden agendas come to light, threatening to tear apart the very fabric of their existence.

"The Tapestry of Honesty: Unraveling Deceit in the Family," is a riveting tale of love, betrayal, and redemption, where the lines between right and wrong blur, and the consequences of deceit reverberate throughout generations. Join us as we embark on a journey into the heart of a family torn apart by lies, and discover the power of honesty to heal even the deepest of wounds.

About The Author

Thangjam Ramananda Singh is a seasoned tax consultant, accomplished author, and advocate for cultural exploration. With a diverse educational background encompassing a Bachelor of Science (BSc), Bachelor of Laws (LLB), and Post Graduate Diploma in Business Management (PGDBM), Singh brings a unique blend of expertise to his writing endeavors.

Drawing from his professional experience and passion for literature, Singh has authored several thought-provoking books that delve into a wide array of subjects. His works include "Other's Judgement of You," which explores the intricacies of human perception and social dynamics, and "When I Touch," a poignant exploration of sensory experiences and emotional connections.

In "Money: The Root of Crime," Singh delves into the complex relationship between financial disparities and criminal activities, offering insightful commentary on societal issues. Additionally, Singh serves as an ambassador for his home state of Manipur through his book "Come Explore Manipur Hidden Treasures: Manipur Tourism," where he invites readers to discover the cultural richness and hidden gems of this vibrant region.

With each publication, Thangjam Ramananda Singh showcases his versatility as an author and his commitment to fostering understanding and appreciation across diverse subject matters.

CHAPTER ONE

INTRODUCTION

A. Introduce Luther and Melody, a couple grappling with the challenges of parenthood.

Luther and Melody are a couple deeply entrenched in the journey of parenthood, each grappling with their own set of challenges and triumphs as they navigate the intricacies of raising their two sons, Roger and Rupesh. Luther, a diligent and hardworking man, takes great pride in providing for his family. He works long hours to ensure that they have everything they need, often sacrificing his desires for the sake of his loved ones. However, beneath his stoic exterior lies a sense of uncertainty, as he grapples with the constant demands placed upon him by his sons and the strain it places on their family dynamic.

Melody, on the other hand, is the heart and soul of the family. Her warm and nurturing nature makes her the pillar of strength that holds their household together. She approaches parenthood with unwavering dedication, striving to create a loving and supportive environment for her children to thrive in. Yet, behind her gentle demeanor,

Melody harbors her fears and insecurities, struggling to balance her maternal instincts with the harsh realities of everyday life. Luther and Melody form a formidable team, united by their shared commitment to their family's well-being. They navigate the highs and lows of parenthood with grace and resilience, finding solace in each other's embrace amidst the chaos of raising two energetic boys. As they confront the challenges of parenthood head-on, Luther and Melody's bond grows stronger, their love for each other serving as a beacon of hope in the face of adversity. Despite the trials they face, they remain steadfast in their determination to provide a bright future for their children, guided by the unwavering belief that together, they can overcome any obstacle that comes their way.

A. Set the stage for a story exploring their family's honesty and deceit dynamics.

In the bustling suburban neighborhood where Luther and Melody reside, the stage is set for a story that delves deep into the intricate dynamics of honesty and deceit within their family. On the surface, their home exudes warmth and familiarity, with a neatly manicured lawn and a cozy front porch adorned with colorful flower pots. Inside, the walls are adorned with family photos capturing precious moments of laughter and love. But beneath this façade of domestic bliss lies a tangled web of secrets and half-truths that threaten to unravel the very fabric of their family unit.

As Luther and Melody navigate the challenges of parenthood, they find themselves grappling with the constant demands placed upon them by their two sons, Roger and Rupesh. The boys, though seemingly innocent in their youthful exuberance, harbor their hidden agendas, constantly seeking ways to manipulate their parents into fulfilling their desires. Roger, the eldest son, is charming and charismatic, with a knack for getting what he wants through the art of persuasion and manipulation. He knows just the right words to say to tug at his parents' heartstrings, weaving intricate lies to justify his every whim and desire. Meanwhile, Rupesh, the younger of the two, is more reserved and introspective, often overshadowed by his older brother's flamboyant personality. Yet, beneath his quiet exterior lies a cunning intellect and a talent for deception that rivals even Roger's.

As Luther and Melody attempt to decipher the truth amidst a sea of lies, they find themselves caught in a constant battle of wills with their sons. Each day brings new challenges as they struggle to discern fact from fiction, questioning their instincts and grappling with feelings of betrayal and mistrust. But amidst the chaos, Luther and Melody cling to the hope that honesty will prevail, believing that they can overcome the deceit that threatens to tear their family apart through open communication and unwavering love. Little do they know, however, that the roots of deception run deeper than they could ever imagine, stretching far beyond the confines of their own home and into the very heart of their community. As the story unfolds, Luther and Melody are forced to confront the harsh realities of their family's secrets, navigating a treacherous journey of self-discovery and redemption. Along the way, they will learn that the path to truth is fraught with obstacles, but with perseverance and determination, they may just find their way back to each other, stronger and more united than ever before.

THE FAMILY DYNAMIC

A. Describe Luther and Melody's daily struggles to meet the demands of their two sons, Roger and Rupesh.

As Luther and Melody navigate the chaotic morning routine, they exchange weary glances, silently acknowledging the challenges they face in meeting their sons' demands. Luther scrambles eggs while Melody toasts bread, trying to keep up with Roger and Rupesh's picky eating habits. Despite their best efforts to provide nutritious meals, they often find themselves at odds with their sons' ever-changing preferences and dietary restrictions. Roger's insistence on his favorite cereal with a specific type of milk adds another layer of complexity to the morning rush. Melody searches through the pantry, hoping to find the last box of cereal hidden behind the oatmeal and granola. Meanwhile, Luther juggles multiple tasks at once, attempting to brew coffee while flipping pancakes on the stove. In the chaos, Rupesh declares his refusal to eat anything but toast with jam, leaving Melody scrambling to find the loaf of bread amidst the cluttered kitchen counter. Luther and Melody exchange exasperated sighs, feeling the weight of parental responsibility bearing down on them as they struggle to keep up with their sons' demands.

Despite the challenges they face, Luther and Melody persevere, knowing that their efforts to provide for their children's needs are borne out of love and devotion. As they sit down to breakfast together, sharing tired smiles and laughter amidst the chaos, they find solace in the knowledge that their family's bond is stronger than any morning rush or dietary restriction. As Luther and Melody rush to get Roger and Rupesh ready for school, they're met with a familiar plea for money. Roger insists he needs cash for an upcoming school trip, while Rupesh claims he's run out of essential stationery supplies. Luther and Melody exchange worried glances, their suspicions about the boys' true intentions growing stronger with each request. Despite their concerns, Luther and Melody reluctantly hand over the money, hoping to avoid a confrontation in the hectic moments before the day has even begun. They rationalize their decision, telling themselves that they don't want to deprive their sons of opportunities or essentials. However, a nagging sense of unease gnaws at them as they watch Roger and Rupesh hurry off to school.

As they drive away, Luther and Melody can't shake the feeling that they may be enabling their sons' deceptive behavior. They worry about the message they're sending by giving in to their demands without questioning their motives. Deep down, they know that fostering honesty and accountability requires more than just handing out money whenever their sons ask for it. With heavy hearts, Luther and Melody resolve to address the issue head-on, determined to have a candid conversation with Roger and Rupesh about the importance of honesty and responsibility. They realize that while it may be challenging at the moment, confronting their sons' deceptive behavior is essential for nurturing trust and integrity within their family. As they drive home, they steel themselves for the difficult conversation that lies ahead, knowing that it's the first step towards building a stronger, more honest relationship with their sons.

As Luther heads off to work, Melody's day begins with a flurry of activity as she tackles household chores and runs errands. However, her mind is consumed with worry about Roger and Rupesh. The constant stream of requests for money only adds to her stress, as she receives a text from Roger asking for funds to buy lunch, followed by a phone call from Rupesh requesting money for a school project. Despite feeling overwhelmed by their relentless demands, Melody can't shake the nagging sense of guilt that accompanies her inability to provide for her sons' needs without question. She knows that giving in to their requests only perpetuates their deceptive behavior, yet she can't help but feel torn between wanting to meet their needs and wanting to teach them the value of honesty and responsibility.

As the day wears on, Melody finds herself consumed by anxiety, wondering what lies her sons may be hiding from her. She replays their requests for money in her mind, searching for clues or inconsistencies that might reveal the truth behind their motives. With each passing hour, her worry intensifies, as she grapples with the weight of uncertainty and the fear of what secrets her sons may be keeping from her. Despite her fears, Melody knows that she must confront the issue head-on and address her sons' deceptive behavior. She resolves to have a candid conversation with Roger and Rupesh when they return home from school, emphasizing the importance of honesty and accountability in their family. As she prepares for their arrival, Melody steel herself for the difficult conversation ahead, knowing that it's the first step towards building a stronger, more honest relationship with her sons.

As Luther returns home from work, tensions within the household reach a boiling point as Roger and Rupesh present their latest requests for money. Luther and Melody, weary from a day filled with worry and anxiety, try to reason with the boys, questioning the necessity of their purchases and urging them to be honest about their intentions. However, Roger and Rupesh's evasive responses only fuel their parents' suspicions, leading to a heated argument that threatens to tear the family apart. Luther and Melody feel frustration and disappointment mounting as they struggle to understand why their sons continue to resort to deception. They implore Roger and Rupesh to consider the consequences of their actions and the impact it has on their family, but their pleas fall on deaf ears. The atmosphere becomes charged with emotion as accusations fly back and forth, leaving Luther and Melody feeling helpless and defeated.

Despite their best efforts to maintain peace, Luther and Melody find themselves at a loss, unsure of how to break free from the cycle of deceit that has gripped their family. They realize that they can no longer ignore the issue or sweep it under the rug. It's a pivotal moment that forces them to confront the harsh reality of their situation and take decisive action to address the underlying issues at hand. With heavy hearts, Luther and Melody resolve to seek outside help and guidance, recognizing that they cannot navigate this challenge alone. They reach out to trusted friends, family members, or professionals for support, determined to work together as a family to overcome the obstacles that stand in their way. As they embark on this journey of healing and reconciliation, Luther and Melody cling to the hope that through honesty, communication, and perseverance, they can emerge stronger and more united than ever before.

As the day comes to a close, Luther and Melody find themselves engulfed in the emotional aftermath of their sons' deception. The weight of disappointment and frustration hangs heavy in the air as they grapple with the unsettling realization that their family is in crisis. They question their parenting abilities, wondering where they went wrong and how they can set their family back on the right path. With each passing moment, the burden of their sons' lies grows heavier, threatening to crush the fragile bonds that hold their family together. Luther and Melody feel a sense of despair wash over them as they struggle to make sense of the chaos unfolding within their home. They search for answers in the depths of their hearts, hoping to find a glimmer of hope amidst the darkness that surrounds them.

As they retire to bed, exhaustion washes over Luther and Melody, both physically and emotionally drained from the day's events. They lie awake in the darkness, their minds consumed by worries and fears about what tomorrow will bring. They wonder whether they will ever find a way to break free from the suffocating cycle of dishonesty that has consumed their lives and whether they will ever be able to repair the shattered trust within their family. Despite the uncertainty that looms over them, Luther and Melody cling to a sliver of hope, knowing that their love for each other and their sons will guide them through the darkest of times. They vow to face the challenges ahead with courage and resilience, determined to rebuild their family on a foundation of honesty, trust, and unconditional love. As they drift off into a troubled sleep, they cling to the belief that with time and perseverance, they will find a way to overcome the obstacles that stand in their way and emerge stronger and more united than ever before.

B. Highlight the influence of Luther's father, Robert, on the family's values and behaviors.

In the opening chapter, Luther's father, Robert, emerges as a central figure in the family's narrative. Luther and Melody reminisce about their upbringing, sharing nostalgic anecdotes and fond memories that highlight Robert's profound influence on their lives. Through these stories, the reader gains insight into Robert's character and the values he instilled in Luther and Melody. Robert is portrayed as a pillar of strength and wisdom, whose presence looms large in Luther's childhood memories. He is described as a man of integrity and principle, whose actions speak louder than words. Luther and Melody recall moments of guidance and support from Robert, as he imparted valuable life lessons and taught them the importance of honesty, hard work, and perseverance.

As Luther reflects on his journey as a parent, he finds himself drawing upon the lessons learned from his father. He strives to emulate Robert's example, seeking to instill the same values of integrity and responsibility in his children. Melody, too, looks to Robert as a source of inspiration, recognizing the impact he had on shaping her husband's character and outlook on life. Throughout the opening chapter, Robert's presence serves as a guiding light for Luther and Melody as they navigate the complexities of parenthood. His legacy lives on through the values he imparted to his children, reminding them of the importance of family, love, and integrity in the face of life's challenges. As the story unfolds, Robert's influence continues to resonate, shaping the choices and decisions of the characters as they strive to uphold the principles he holds dear.

As Luther and Melody navigate the complexities of parenthood, they turn to Robert, Luther's father and a beacon of wisdom, for guidance. In this pivotal chapter, Robert becomes a source of invaluable insight as he imparts his wisdom on family values and behavior, drawing from his own experiences as a parent and grandparent. Through heartfelt conversations and shared reflections, Robert's influence on Luther and Melody's parenting style becomes evident. He shares anecdotes and lessons learned from raising Luther and his siblings, offering practical advice on fostering trust, communication, and mutual respect within the family.

Robert emphasizes the importance of leading by example and setting clear boundaries, encouraging Luther and Melody to be consistent and firm in their approach to discipline. He underscores the value of open and honest communication, urging them to create a safe and nurturing environment where their sons feel comfortable expressing themselves. As Luther and Melody listen to Robert's words of wisdom, they are inspired to reassess their parenting practices and make adjustments where necessary. They recognize the significance of instilling strong moral values and a sense of responsibility in their children, just as

Robert did with them.

Robert's presence serves as a guiding light for Luther and Melody as they navigate the challenges of raising their sons. His timeless advice and unwavering support instill them with confidence and determination, empowering them to confront the complexities of parenthood with grace and resilience. Luther and Melody emerge with a renewed sense of purpose and clarity, armed with the knowledge and wisdom passed down from Robert. With his guidance, they feel better equipped to navigate the ups and downs of parenting and to nurture a loving and supportive family environment for Roger and Rupesh. Robert's influence continues to shape their decisions and interactions, serving as a constant reminder of the enduring power of family values and the importance of generational wisdom in shaping the future.

As Luther and Melody delve deeper into the generational patterns that have shaped their family dynamic, Robert's influence becomes even more pronounced. Through heartfelt discussions with Robert, they begin to unravel the recurring themes and behaviors that have been passed down through the generations, shedding light on the underlying factors that have contributed to their current struggles. Robert serves as a repository of wisdom and experience, offering invaluable insights into the family's history and the patterns of behavior that have persisted over time. He shares anecdotes and stories from his upbringing, revealing how certain attitudes and beliefs were passed down from one generation to the next. Luther and Melody listen intently, recognizing parallels between their own experiences and those of their ancestors.

As Luther and Melody confront these patterns head-on, they are inspired by Robert's wisdom and guidance to break free from destructive cycles and forge a new path forward for their family. They realize that to create lasting change, they must first acknowledge and understand the roots of their behavior, confronting the legacy of dishonesty and mistrust that has plagued their family for generations. With Robert's support, Luther and Melody embark on a journey of self-discovery and transformation, challenging long-held beliefs and assumptions about what it means to be a family. They begin to question the narratives that have shaped their lives, daring to imagine a future where honesty, trust, and love prevail over deceit and betrayal.

Through their discussions with Robert, Luther, and Melody come to realize that they have the power to rewrite the story of their family, break free from the chains of the past, and create a new legacy of integrity and authenticity. With Robert's guidance, they embrace the opportunity to chart a new course, one built on a foundation of honesty, trust, and mutual respect. As they continue their journey, Luther and Melody are filled with hope and determination, knowing that with Robert's support and guidance, they can overcome any obstacle and build a brighter future for themselves and their children. Robert's influence remains a guiding force in their lives, inspiring them to embrace change and embrace the possibility of a new beginning for their family.

Robert takes on the role of a catalyst for change within the family as he challenges Luther and Melody's perspectives on honesty and integrity. Through thought-provoking conversations and probing questions, he encourages them to examine their values and beliefs, urging them to prioritize honesty and transparency in their interactions with one another. Robert's unwavering commitment to these principles serves as a guiding light for Luther and Melody as they grapple with the complexities of parenthood. He shares personal anecdotes and life lessons, illustrating the profound impact that honesty and integrity have had on his own life and relationships. Through his words, Robert instills in Luther and Melody a deeper appreciation for the importance of these values in fostering trust and mutual respect within the family.

As Luther and Melody engage in dialogue with Robert, they are forced to confront their shortcomings and biases. His probing questions challenge them to reassess their priorities and reassess their approach to parenting, prompting them to consider how their actions and words impact their sons' perception of honesty and integrity. Through Robert's guidance, Luther and Melody begin to recognize the ripple effect of their behavior on their family dynamic. They realize that by prioritizing honesty and transparency, they can create a safe and nurturing environment where open communication thrives, laying the foundation for stronger, more authentic relationships with their sons.

Robert's influence has sparked a profound transformation within the family. Luther and Melody emerge with a renewed sense of purpose and determination, committed to fostering a culture of honesty and integrity within their home. Inspired by Robert's unwavering commitment to these principles, they embark on a journey of self-discovery and growth, embracing the opportunity to create a brighter future for themselves and their children.

As the story progresses, Robert's influence on the family values and behavior becomes more pronounced as Luther and Melody strive to strengthen their bonds with their children. Through Robert's guidance, they learn the importance of nurturing open communication and fostering a sense of trust and understanding within the family. Robert's unwavering support and encouragement empower Luther and Melody to embrace their roles as parents with confidence and conviction, laying the foundation for a brighter future for their family. Robert's influence on the family values and behavior is woven seamlessly into the narrative, enriching the story with depth and complexity. Through his wisdom, guidance, and unwavering support, Robert serves as a pillar of strength for Luther and Melody, inspiring them to embrace their roles as parents with courage and determination.

CHAPTER THREE

THE CYCLE OF DECEPTION

A. Roger and Rupesh's constant requests for money reveal a pattern of dishonesty within the family.

The story opens with Luther and Melody's usual morning hustle, a routine disrupted by the persistent requests for money from their sons, Roger and Rupesh. Roger asserts he needs cash for an imminent school trip, while Rupesh insists he's depleted his stationery supplies. Initially, Luther and Melody, absorbed in the rush of the morning, don't suspect any deceit. However, as the requests become more frequent and increasingly frivolous, they start to notice a troubling pattern emerging. With each new demand for money, Luther and Melody's exchange concerned glances, a growing unease settling in their stomachs. They recall similar instances in the past, instances where their sons' supposed needs turned out to be veiled for their wants. Roger's seemingly essential school trip expenses and Rupesh's sudden shortage of stationery raise red flags in Luther and Melody's minds.

Despite their doubts, Luther and Melody hesitate to confront their sons, fearing conflict and tension in the already hectic morning rush. Instead, they reluctantly hand over the money, hoping to keep the peace and avoid further disruption. Yet, a lingering sense of unease persists as they bid Roger and Rupesh goodbye, their minds plagued by questions about the true motives behind their sons' requests. As Luther and Melody go about their day, the nagging suspicion refuses to fade. They find themselves pondering the significance of the pattern they've observed, wondering whether their sons' constant demands for money are symptomatic of a deeper issue. With each passing hour, the weight of uncertainty grows heavier, casting a shadow over their once-peaceful household.

The story sets the stage for a journey of introspection and discovery as Luther and Melody grapple with the implications of their son's behavior. With the realization that something is amiss, they are compelled to delve deeper into the root cause of the deceit, confronting uncomfortable truths and facing difficult conversations that threaten to upend their family dynamic. As Luther and Melody delve deeper into Roger and Rupesh's demands for money, they begin to uncover inconsistencies in their sons' stories. Roger's purported school trip, which initially seemed like a legitimate expense, turns out to be a casual day out with friends. Similarly, Rupesh's alleged need for stationery supplies is debunked when Luther and Melody discover a well-stocked desk drawer in his room.

The discovery of these discrepancies sends shock waves through Luther and Melody's world, shattering the illusion of trust and reliability they had placed in their sons. Suspicion mounts as they confront Roger and Rupesh about the inconsistencies, their hearts heavy with disappointment and betrayal. However, their sons' responses only serve to reinforce the pattern of dishonesty within the family. Roger and Rupesh offer flimsy excuses and deflective explanations, refusing to take responsibility for their actions or acknowledge the impact of their deceit. Luther and Melody are left feeling frustrated and powerless, unsure of how to navigate the turbulent waters of their fractured family dynamic.

As tensions rise and emotions run high, Luther and Melody grapple with the painful realization that their sons have been lying to them, possibly for quite some time. They struggle to reconcile the image of their loving, trustworthy children with the reality of their deceptive behavior, grappling with feelings of hurt, betrayal, and disappointment. Despite their best efforts to maintain a sense of composure, Luther and Melody find themselves overwhelmed by a flood of conflicting emotions. They are torn between their desire to protect their sons and their need to address the underlying issues at hand. With each passing moment, the divide between them grows wider, threatening to tear their family apart at the seams.

In the face of adversity, Luther and Melody are forced to confront the harsh truth about their family, knowing that they can no longer turn a blind eye to the lies and deceit that have infiltrated their lives. As they stand at the crossroads of uncertainty, they realize that the path forward will be fraught with challenges and obstacles, but they are determined to face them head-on, armed with the strength of their love and the resolve to rebuild what has been broken. As tensions reach a boiling point, Luther and Melody can no longer ignore the elephant in the room. They confront Roger and Rupesh about their dishonest behavior, their voices trembling with a mixture of anger, disappointment, and sorrow. Despite their sons' attempts to justify their actions, Luther and Melody's unwavering resolve to get to the truth only intensifies.

Roger and Rupesh's lies unravel under the scrutiny of their parents' probing questions, revealing the extent of their deception. Luther and Melody are shocked and dismayed as the full scope of their sons' dishonesty comes to light. The betrayal cuts deep, leaving them reeling from the realization that their trust has been betrayed by those they held most dear. Roger and Rupesh's attempts to deflect blame and downplay the severity of their actions only serve to exacerbate the tension in the room. Luther and Melody refuse to back down, insisting on accountability and transparency from their sons. The air crackles with emotion as accusations fly back and forth, the once-solid foundation of their family shaken to its core.

Despite the heartache and turmoil, Luther and Melody remain steadfast in their determination to address the issue head-on. They refuse to sweep their sons' deceit under the rug or pretend that everything is okay. Instead, they confront the uncomfortable truths and face the consequences of their sons' actions with courage and resilience. As the dust settles and the initial shock begins to fade, Luther and Melody are left to pick up the pieces of their shattered family dynamic. The road ahead may be long and arduous, but they know that they must confront the issue now to heal and rebuild trust within their family. With each passing moment, their resolve only grows stronger, fueled by the love and determination to overcome the challenges that lie ahead.

As the repercussions of Roger and Rupesh's dishonesty reverberate throughout the household, Luther and Melody grapple with feelings of betrayal and mistrust. The once-close bond between parent and child is strained as Luther and Melody struggle to come to terms with the realization that their sons have been lying to them. The family dynamic is thrown into disarray as Luther and Melody attempt to navigate the fallout of their sons' actions and rebuild trust in their relationship. With emotions running high, Luther and Melody seek solutions to address the pattern of dishonesty within their family. They engage in open and honest communication with Roger and Rupesh, encouraging them to take responsibility for their actions and make amends for the hurt they have caused. Through heartfelt conversations and mutual understanding, Luther and Melody begin the process of healing and reconciliation, laying the groundwork for a more transparent and authentic family dynamic moving forward.

Roger and Rupesh's constant requests for money catalyze exploring the theme of dishonesty within the family. As Luther and Melody confront the issue head-on, they are forced to confront uncomfortable truths about themselves and their children, ultimately leading to a deeper understanding of the importance of honesty and integrity in their relationships.

B. Luther and Melody's attempts to question their sons' motives are met with evasive responses and half-truths.

Luther and Melody's suspicion mounts as they notice inconsistencies in Roger and Rupesh's requests for money. They begin to question their sons about their motives, seeking clarification on why they need the funds and how they plan to use them. However, Roger and Rupesh's responses only deepen their concern. As Luther and

Melody press for answers, they are met with vague explanations and evasive responses from their sons. Roger and Rupesh deflect the questions, avoiding direct answers and skirting around the issue at hand. Their nonchalant demeanor and lack of transparency only serve to fuel Luther and Melody's growing unease.

Despite their sons' attempts to brush off their concerns, Luther and Melody refuse to ignore the nagging suspicion gnawing at them. They know that something isn't adding up, and they are determined to get to the bottom of it. With each evasive response, their resolve to uncover the truth strengthens, driving them to delve deeper into the mystery surrounding their son's behavior. As Luther and Melody continue to question Roger and Rupesh, the tension in the air becomes palpable. The once-harmonious atmosphere of their home is now clouded by uncertainty and mistrust. Luther and Melody can't help but feel a sense of betrayal as they realize their sons may not be telling them the whole truth.

Despite the discomfort of confronting their sons, Luther and Melody know that they must persevere in their quest for answers. They refuse to turn a blind eye to the deceit unfolding before them, knowing that honesty and transparency are the cornerstones of a healthy family dynamic. With each passing moment, their determination to uncover the truth only grows stronger, propelling them forward in their pursuit of clarity and resolution. As Roger and Rupesh's evasive responses become more frequent, Luther and Melody's suspicions are heightened to a point of deep concern. They become increasingly wary of their sons' motives, sensing that something isn't quite right with their behavior. Luther and Melody begin to scrutinize their sons' actions and words more closely, searching for any hint of deception or dishonesty.

Despite their best efforts to get to the bottom of the issue, Roger and Rupesh persist in offering half-truths and excuses. Their responses are evasive and inconsistent, leaving Luther and Melody feeling frustrated and perplexed. With each passing interaction, Luther and Melody's concerns about their sons' honesty and integrity grow more pronounced. Luther and Melody find themselves caught in a web of uncertainty, unsure of how to navigate the increasingly complex situation with their sons. They feel torn between wanting to believe in their sons' innocence and facing the harsh reality of their deceptive behavior. The once-solid foundation of trust within their family begins to crumble, leaving Luther and Melody feeling adrift in a sea of doubt and suspicion.

Despite the challenges they face, Luther and Melody refuse to give up on their quest for the truth. They remain steadfast in their determination to confront Roger and Rupesh about their dishonesty, knowing that they must address the issue head-on to restore trust and integrity within their family. With each evasive response from their sons, Luther and Melody's resolve only strengthens, fueling their determination to uncover the secrets that lie beneath the surface of their seemingly idyllic family life.

Frustrated by their sons' continued evasiveness, Luther and Melody reach a breaking point and decide to confront Roger and Rupesh directly. They gather their sons together and express their concerns about the pattern of dishonesty they have observed, leaving no room for ambiguity or excuses. Luther and Melody demand honest answers from their sons, insisting that they deserve to know the truth. However, instead of admitting to their deceit, Roger and Rupesh become defensive and attempt to justify their behavior. They offer a slew of excuses and explanations, insisting that they have valid reasons for their actions. Despite Luther and Melody's insistence on transparency and accountability, Roger and Rupesh refuse to take responsibility for their dishonesty, further exacerbating the tension in the room.

Luther and Melody are left feeling conflicted and uncertain as they grapple with their sons' unwillingness to come clean. They had hoped for a resolution, a moment of honesty and reconciliation that would pave the way for healing and understanding within their family. Instead, they are met with resistance and defiance, leaving them feeling more lost and disillusioned than ever before. As the confrontation draws to a close, Luther and Melody are left to wrestle with the fallout of their sons' dishonesty. They feel a sense of betrayal and disappointment, wondering where they went wrong as parents and how they can mend the fractured trust within their family. With each passing moment, the divide between them and their sons seems to widen, leaving Luther and Melody feeling more isolated and alone than ever before.

As Roger and Rupesh's evasive responses persist, Luther and Melody come to a sobering realization: their sons may be hiding something from them. The pattern of deceit and avoidance has become too blatant to ignore, and Luther and Melody can no longer deny the possibility that their sons may not trust them enough to be honest about their intentions. This realization strikes a painful blow, leaving Luther and Melody grappling with feelings of hurt and betrayal. The foundation of trust upon which their family was built now feels fragile and unstable. Luther and Melody had always believed in open communication and honesty within their household, but now they are faced with the harsh reality that their sons may be keeping secrets from them. The thought that Roger and Rupesh may not feel comfortable confiding in them wounds Luther and Melody deeply, shaking their confidence as parents and leaving them questioning where they went wrong.

Despite their disappointment and heartache, Luther and Melody refuse to succumb to despair. They are determined to uncover the truth and address the underlying issues driving their sons' deceitful behavior. With each passing day, their resolve only strengthens, fueled by their unwavering commitment to their family and their belief that honesty and trust are worth fighting for. Luther and Melody know that they have a long and difficult road ahead of them, but they are willing to do whatever it takes to rebuild the trust that has been broken. They cling to the hope that through open communication and unconditional love, they can bridge the gap that has formed between them and their sons. With determination in their hearts, Luther and Melody steel themselves for the challenges that lie ahead, ready to confront the truth and rebuild their family stronger than ever before.

Luther and Melody refuse to give up on their quest to address their sons' evasiveness and half-truths. Despite the challenges they face, they remain determined to find solutions to rebuild trust and transparency within their family. With a renewed sense of purpose, Luther and Melody explore different approaches to communication and conflict resolution. They recognize that fostering open and honest dialogue is key to resolving the underlying issues driving Roger and Rupesh's deceitful behavior. They commit themselves to creating a safe and supportive environment where their sons feel comfortable expressing their feelings and intentions without fear of judgment or retribution.

Luther and Melody engage Roger and Rupesh in heartfelt conversations, encouraging them to be more forthcoming about their experiences and struggles. They listen attentively, offering support and guidance as their sons navigate the complexities of adolescence and self-discovery. Through patience and understanding, Luther and Melody hope to bridge the gap that has formed between them and their sons, laying the groundwork for a more authentic and trusting relationship moving forward. As the days pass, Luther and Melody begin to see signs of progress. Roger and Rupesh slowly open up about their feelings and experiences, sharing their hopes, fears, and dreams with newfound honesty and vulnerability. Luther and Melody cherish these moments of connection, knowing that they are a testament to the resilience of their family bond.

With each honest conversation, Luther and Melody feel a sense of hope and optimism for the future. They know that rebuilding trust and transparency within their family will take time and effort, but they are committed to doing whatever it takes to heal the wounds that have been inflicted. Together, they embrace the journey ahead, knowing that with love, patience, and understanding, their family can emerge stronger and more united than ever before.

CHAPTER FOUR

THE BLURRED LINES OF TRUTH

A. Explore the origins of Roger and Rupesh's deceptive behavior, questioning whether it stems from parental influence or innate tendencies.

The story opens with Luther and Melody observing early signs of deceptive behavior in their sons, Roger and Rupesh. The couple shares a moment of reflection, wondering if they may have unwittingly contributed to their sons' tendencies through their parenting styles. Luther recalls moments when he may have dismissed small lies from the boys, attributing them to harmless childhood imagination. He remembers times when Roger and Rupesh embellished stories or exaggerated the truth, and he now wonders if he should have addressed these behaviors more directly.

Similarly, Melody reflects on instances where she may have overlooked inconsistencies in her sons' stories, believing them to be innocent mistakes. She recalls times when Roger and Rupesh may have omitted important details or avoided answering questions directly, and she questions whether she should have probed further into their explanations. As Luther and Melody discuss their concerns, they grapple with the question of whether Roger and Rupesh's deceptive behavior stems from parental influence or innate tendencies. They wonder if they may have inadvertently set a precedent for dishonesty by not addressing their sons' behaviors more firmly in the past.

The couple recognizes the importance of taking responsibility for their role in shaping their sons' characters and behaviors. They resolve to be more vigilant in addressing any signs of dishonesty in the future, and they commit to fostering a culture of honesty and integrity within their family. With a newfound awareness of the potential impact of their parenting choices, Luther and Melody embark on a journey of self-reflection and growth. They are determined to understand the root causes of Roger and Rupesh's deceptive behavior and to guide them toward a path of honesty and transparency.

As Luther and Melody delve deeper into the origins of Roger and Rupesh's deceptive behavior, they broaden their perspective to consider the various environmental factors that may have contributed to their sons' tendencies. They explore the intricacies of their family dynamics, peer influences, and societal pressures, seeking to understand how these external factors have shaped their sons' attitudes toward honesty and deceit. Reflecting on their upbringing, Luther and Melody contemplate the values instilled in them by their parents and the impact of these influences on their behavior. They recall the lessons they learned about honesty, integrity, and moral responsibility, and they wonder whether similar influences have shaped Roger and Rupesh's behavior.

Luther and Melody also consider the role of peer influences in shaping their sons' attitudes toward honesty and deceit. They reflect on the friends Roger and Rupesh spend time with and the potential influence these relationships may have on their sons' behavior. They wonder if peer pressure or a desire to fit in with their social circle has led Roger and Rupesh to engage in deceptive behavior. Additionally, Luther and Melody examine the broader societal pressures that may have contributed to their sons' tendencies toward dishonesty. They consider the messages about success, achievement, and self-worth that permeate modern society and how these messages may influence Roger and Rupesh's behavior.

As they contemplate these various factors, Luther and Melody recognize the complexity of their son's behavior and the multitude of influences that may have contributed to it. They are determined to address these underlying issues and guide Roger and Rupesh toward a path of honesty and integrity, but they know that it will require patience, understanding, and a willingness to confront uncomfortable truths about themselves and their family. Luther and Melody find themselves immersed in the age-old debate of nature versus nurture as they strive to unravel the complexities of Roger and Rupesh's deceptive behavior. They delve into research on genetic predispositions and psychological theories of personality development, seeking insights into whether their sons' tendencies towards dishonesty are inherent traits or learned behaviors.

As they pore over scientific studies and academic literature, Luther and Melody weigh the evidence for and against the influence of genetics on their sons' behavior. They consider the possibility that Roger and Rupesh may have inherited certain personality traits or predispositions towards deception from their biological parents, despite their best efforts to provide a nurturing and supportive environment At the same time, Luther and Melody reflect on their personalities and behavioral traits, wondering if they have unwittingly passed down certain characteristics to their children. They examine their tendencies towards honesty and deceit, searching for clues to their sons' behavior in their own experiences and upbringing.

The couple engages in deep introspection, questioning whether their parenting style or family dynamics may have inadvertently contributed to Roger and Rupesh's deceptive tendencies. They grapple with feelings of guilt and self-doubt, wondering if they could have done more to instill a sense of integrity and honesty in their sons. As they navigate the complexities of nature versus nurture, Luther and Melody are faced with difficult questions and uncomfortable truths about themselves and their family. Yet, they remain steadfast in their determination to understand the root causes of their sons' behavior and to guide them toward a path of honesty and integrity. With each new revelation and insight, they inch closer to unraveling the mystery of Roger and Rupesh's deceptive behavior, and to finding the solutions that will help their family heal and grow stronger together.

As Luther and Melody engage in introspection, they confront their fears and insecurities about their parenting practices. They grapple with questions about their ability to raise honest and trustworthy children, questioning whether they have been consistent in enforcing consequences for dishonesty and providing a positive role model for their sons. The couple engages in candid discussions about their strengths and weaknesses as parents, acknowledging that they may have inadvertently contributed to Roger and Rupesh's deceptive behavior. They reflect on moments when they may have turned a blind eye to small lies or failed to address inconsistencies in their sons' stories, realizing that these missed opportunities may have reinforced their sons' deceptive tendencies.

Luther and Melody wrestle with feelings of guilt and self-doubt, wondering if they have failed their sons in some way. They question whether they have provided a nurturing and supportive environment where honesty and integrity are valued and rewarded, or if they have inadvertently created an atmosphere where deception is tolerated and even encouraged. As they confront these difficult truths, Luther and Melody are forced to reckon with their imperfections as parents. They recognize that raising children is a complex and challenging endeavor, filled with moments of doubt and uncertainty. Yet, they refuse to succumb to despair, knowing that they have the power to make positive changes and guide their sons toward a path of honesty and integrity.

With renewed determination, Luther and Melody commit themselves to being more vigilant in addressing dishonesty and reinforcing positive values within their family. They pledge to lead by example, demonstrating honesty, integrity, and accountability in their own words and actions. As they embark on this journey of self-improvement and growth, they hold onto the hope that with love, patience, and perseverance, they can help Roger and Rupesh overcome their deceptive tendencies and become the honest and trustworthy individuals they aspire to be.

As Luther and Melody grapple with the complexity of their sons' deceptive behavior, they come to a profound realization: it is likely a combination of parental influence and innate tendencies that have shaped Roger and Rupesh's attitudes towards honesty and deceit. They recognize that while they may have played a role in reinforcing certain behaviors, their sons' actions are also influenced by their personalities and experiences. Despite their concerns, Luther and Melody refuse to give up on their sons. They are determined to support Roger and Rupesh through their struggles and help them develop a stronger sense of integrity and accountability. They understand that this will require patience, understanding, and unwavering support, but they are willing to do whatever it takes to guide their sons toward a healthier and more honest path.

Luther and Melody commit themselves to fostering open communication and trust within their family. They create a safe and supportive environment where Roger and Rupesh feel comfortable expressing themselves and sharing their thoughts and feelings. They encourage their sons to be honest and transparent, reassuring them that they will always be there to listen and offer guidance without judgment. As they embark on this journey of growth and self-discovery, Luther and Melody hold onto the hope that their efforts will pay off in the long run. They understand that change won't happen overnight, but they are committed to laying the groundwork for a healthier and more honest relationship with Roger and Rupesh in the future. With love, patience, and perseverance, they believe that their family can overcome any obstacle and emerge stronger than ever before.

B. Highlight similar patterns of deceit within the neighboring family, suggesting a broader societal issue.

The story commences with Luther and Melody keenly observing parallels between the deceptive behaviors of their sons, Roger and Rupesh, and those of their neighbors' children. They witness how the neighboring family's kids also regularly seek money under pretenses, mirroring the challenges they face with Roger and Rupesh. This shared struggle sparks a sense of curiosity and concern within Luther and Melody. As they delve deeper into their observations, Luther and Melody begin to reflect on the broader societal issues that may be fueling the prevalence of deceit within their community. They ponder the influence of external factors such as peer pressure, media portrayal of success, and societal expectations on the behavior of children and families alike.

Through their contemplation, Luther and Melody come to realize that the challenges they face with Roger and Rupesh may not be unique to their own family but rather symptomatic of larger societal trends. They recognize the importance of addressing these underlying issues not only within their household but also within their community as a whole. Motivated by their observations and insights, Luther and Melody are determined to take action. They resolve to foster open dialogue and collaboration with their neighbors, seeking to address the root causes of deceit and mistrust within their community. Together, they embark on a journey of self-reflection and collective effort, aiming to create a more honest and transparent environment for their families to thrive.

As Luther and Melody engage in more frequent interactions with their neighbors, they uncover common threads that connect their experiences with those of other families in the neighborhood. Through candid conversations and shared anecdotes, they discover that many parents share similar concerns about their children's deceptive behavior and the challenges it poses to their family dynamics. As they delve deeper into these discussions, Luther and Melody begin to realize that deceit may be a widespread issue within their community. They recognize that their own experiences with Roger and Rupesh are not isolated incidents but rather part of a larger pattern affecting multiple families in the neighborhood.

This revelation prompts Luther and Melody to consider the possibility of deeper underlying societal factors at play. They ponder the influence of external pressures such as social media, peer relationships, and academic stressors on the behavior of children in their community. They also question the role of parental expectations and family dynamics in shaping their children's attitudes toward honesty and deceit. As they reflect on these broader societal issues, Luther and Melody become increasingly aware of the need for collective action. They realize that addressing the root causes of deceit within their community will require collaboration and cooperation among families, educators, and community leaders.

Motivated by their newfound understanding, Luther and Melody are inspired to take a proactive approach to addressing the issue of deceit within their neighborhood. They begin to explore strategies for fostering open communication, building trust, and promoting positive values within their community. Through their efforts, they hope to create a more supportive and nurturing environment where families can thrive and children can grow up with integrity and honesty. Luther and Melody engage in conversations with other parents in the neighborhood about their experiences with deceptive behavior in their children. They discuss the challenges they face in addressing the issue and share strategies for fostering honesty and trust within their families. Through these discussions, Luther and Melody gain insight into the broader societal influences that may be contributing to the prevalence of deceit among children in their community.

As Luther and Melody reflect on their conversations with other parents, they begin to connect the dots between their children's deceptive behavior and the broader societal pressures at play. They consider the pervasive influence of media, the complexities of peer relationships, and the subtle impact of cultural norms on their sons' attitudes toward honesty and deceit. With each revelation, Luther and Melody confront the sobering reality that their children are growing up in a world where dishonesty is often rewarded and integrity is undervalued. They recognize the profound impact of social media, where curated personas and exaggerated achievements can distort perceptions of reality and create unrealistic expectations. They also acknowledge the powerful influence of peer relationships, where the pressure to fit in and maintain status can lead to compromising one's values.

Furthermore, Luther and Melody contemplate the role of cultural norms in shaping their children's behavior. They recognize that in a society driven by success and materialism, the temptation to cut corners and bend the truth can be all too enticing. They confront the uncomfortable truth that their children are navigating a world where honesty is sometimes seen as a weakness rather than a virtue. As they grapple with these revelations, Luther and Melody are filled with a sense of urgency to protect their children from the negative influences of society. They vow to remain vigilant and proactive in instilling values of integrity and honesty within their family. They commit to fostering open communication, promoting critical thinking, and modeling ethical behavior for their sons, knowing that these values will serve as their compass in a world where deceit may seem all too commonplace.

Luther and Melody, along with their neighbors, unite in a shared mission to combat the broader societal issues contributing to the prevalence of deceit within their community. Recognizing the urgency of the situation, they come together to advocate for increased awareness and education on the importance of honesty and integrity. As a collective force, Luther, Melody, and their neighbors work tirelessly to raise awareness about the detrimental effects of deceit on individual well-being and community cohesion. They organize workshops, seminars, and community events aimed at empowering parents, educators, and children alike with the knowledge and skills needed to navigate the complexities of honesty in today's world.

Together, they develop and implement initiatives to promote open communication, foster trust, and cultivate a culture of transparency within their families and throughout the wider community. They emphasize the value of ethical decision-making, encouraging individuals to prioritize integrity over personal gain and to take responsibility for their actions. Through their combined efforts, Luther, Melody, and their neighbors hope to create a more transparent and trustworthy environment for their children to grow up in. They understand that building a healthier and more honest society requires a collective commitment to change, and they are determined to lead by example.

As they work towards their shared goal, Luther, Melody, and their neighbors find strength and solidarity in their shared mission. They are inspired by the potential for positive change and motivated by the belief that by working together, they can create a brighter future for their community and generations to come.

THE WEIGHT OF LIES

A. Delve into the emotional toll of maintaining falsehoods within the family, as Luther and Melody struggle with feelings of betrayal and mistrust.

The story opens with Luther and Melody observing subtle inconsistencies in their sons' behavior, triggering a sense of unease within them. They notice small discrepancies in Roger and Rupesh's stories and actions, leading them to suspect that their sons may be deceiving them. However, their reluctance to confront the issue head-on only intensifies their feelings of uncertainty and mistrust. Luther and Melody find themselves caught in a dilemma, torn between their desire to believe in their sons' innocence and their growing suspicions about their honesty. They grapple with the emotional toll of maintaining the facade of a happy family while harboring doubts and suspicions beneath the surface.

As they navigate this internal struggle, Luther and Melody struggle to reconcile their love for their sons with their need for honesty and transparency within their family. They wrestle with feelings of guilt and self-doubt, questioning whether they have failed as parents by not addressing their sons' behavior sooner. Despite their inner turmoil, Luther and Melody are determined to uncover the truth and confront the issue head-on. They understand that avoiding the problem will only prolong their agony and exacerbate the situation. With resolve and determination, they steel themselves for the difficult conversations and tough decisions that lie ahead as they strive to restore trust and integrity within their family.

As Roger and Rupesh's deceptive behavior becomes increasingly evident, Luther and Melody's doubts and disappointments intensify. They find themselves grappling with profound questions about their parenting abilities and where they may have gone wrong in raising their children. Luther and Melody's once unwavering confidence in their sons is shaken to its core as they confront the painful reality that their children may not be the honest and trustworthy individuals they had believed them to be. Feelings of betrayal weigh heavily on Luther and Melody as they struggle to come to terms with the depth of their sons' deceit. They find themselves questioning every decision they've made as parents, agonizing over whether they missed warning signs or failed to instill the values of honesty and integrity in Roger and Rupesh.

The shattered trust between parents and children leaves Luther and Melody feeling vulnerable and exposed, their sense of security undermined by the revelation of their sons' deception. They grapple with a profound sense of loss, mourning the image of the close-knit family they thought they had while facing the harsh reality of their sons' dishonesty. Despite the pain and disillusionment, Luther and Melody are determined to confront the issue head-on and address the underlying causes of their son's behavior. With courage and determination, they vow to rebuild trust and integrity within their family, even as they navigate the turbulent waters of disappointment and betrayal.

As the emotional toll of maintaining falsehoods within the family mounts, Luther and Melody find their relationships with Roger and Rupesh becoming increasingly strained. Communication breaks down as their sons persist in evading their parents' questions and offering half-truths to conceal their deceit. Despite Luther and Melody's attempts to connect with their sons and understand the root of their behavior, they are met with resistance and defensiveness, further exacerbating their feelings of isolation and mistrust. Luther and Melody feel as though they are walking on eggshells around Roger and Rupesh, unsure of how to broach the subject of their sons' dishonesty without inciting anger or denial. They long for the open and honest communication they once shared with their children, but find themselves at a loss as to how to bridge the growing divide between them.

As tensions escalate, Luther and Melody find themselves grappling with feelings of frustration and despair. They yearn to break through the walls their sons have erected around them and rebuild the trust that has been shattered by deception. However, with each passing day, they feel the distance between them and their sons widening, leaving them feeling powerless to mend the fractured bonds of their family. Despite the challenges they face, Luther and Melody refuse to give up hope. They remain steadfast in their commitment to their sons, determined to find a way to reconnect with them and rebuild the foundation of honesty and trust upon which their family is built. With love, patience, and perseverance, they cling to the belief that it is never too late to mend broken relationships and heal the wounds caused by deceit.

Luther and Melody grapple with their internal struggles as they come to terms with the reality of their sons' deceptive behavior. They wrestle with conflicting emotions, torn between their love for their children and their disappointment in their actions. Luther and Melody confront their vulnerabilities and insecurities, wondering if they are to blame for their sons' dishonesty and if they will ever be able to repair the fractured trust between them. As Luther and Melody confront the heavy emotional toll of maintaining falsehoods within their family, they embark on a journey of redemption and healing. They come to understand that to move forward, they must confront the truth head-on and address the underlying issues driving their sons' deceitful behavior.

With a newfound determination, Luther and Melody commit themselves to fostering open and honest communication within their family. They create a safe and supportive environment where Roger and Rupesh feel comfortable expressing themselves and sharing their thoughts and feelings without fear of judgment or retribution. Through heartfelt conversations and heartfelt dialogue, Luther and Melody strive to rebuild trust and repair their relationships with Roger and Rupesh. They acknowledge their shortcomings as parents and apologize for any role they may have played in contributing to their sons' dishonesty.

Together, they work through their past grievances and misunderstandings, laying the groundwork for a brighter and more authentic future. With love, patience, and perseverance, Luther and Melody hold onto the hope that they can mend the fractured bonds of their family and emerge stronger and more united than ever before.

B. Examine the impact of dishonesty on Roger and Rupesh's self-image and relationships with others.

The story opens with Roger and Rupesh engaging in deceptive behavior, spinning intricate webs of lies to manipulate their parents into satisfying their desires. Their actions are driven by a desire for instant gratification and a fear of facing consequences for their actions. As they become more entrenched in their deceitful behavior, Roger and Rupesh begin to internalize the guilt and shame associated with their actions. They wrestle with conflicting emotions, torn between the thrill of getting what they want and the weight of their dishonesty on their conscience.

Their self-image begins to suffer as they grapple with the realization that they are not the honest and trustworthy individuals they once believed themselves to be. They question their worth and integrity, struggling to reconcile their actions with their values and beliefs. Despite their growing feelings of guilt and shame, Roger and Rupesh find themselves trapped in a cycle of deceit, unable to break free from the lies they have woven. As they navigate the consequences of their actions, they come to understand the true cost of dishonesty and the toll it takes on their relationships and sense of self.

As Roger and Rupesh's deceitful behavior persists, they find their relationships with others becoming increasingly strained. They struggle to trust and connect with their family and friends, fearing that their lies will be exposed and their relationships irreparably damaged. Roger and Rupesh's deception creates a barrier between them and those around them, making it difficult for them to form genuine connections or share their true thoughts and feelings. They become increasingly isolated, trapped in a web of lies of their own making.

Their inability to trust others or be honest about their actions only serves to deepen their feelings of loneliness and alienation. They long for acceptance and understanding, but fear that revealing the truth will only further distance them from those they care about. As Roger and Rupesh navigate the consequences of their deceitful behavior, they come to understand the true cost of their actions. They realize that their lies have not only damaged their relationships with others but have also eroded their sense of self-worth and integrity.

Despite their struggles, Roger and Rupesh cling to the hope that they can break free from the cycle of deceit and rebuild the trust they have lost. They understand that it will take time and effort to repair the damage they have done, but are determined to make amends and forge genuine connections based on honesty and mutual respect. The weight of dishonesty bears heavily on Roger and Rupesh's conscience as they grapple with the stark contrast between their actions and their values. They find themselves caught in a relentless tug-of-war between their desire for immediate gain and the nagging pangs of guilt and remorse that accompany their deceitful behavior.

Haunted by the knowledge that their lies have hurt the people they care about most, Roger and Rupesh's sense of self-worth begins to diminish. They struggle to reconcile the image they project to the world with the reality of their actions, grappling with a profound sense of shame and self-doubt. As the consequences of their deceitful behavior begin to unfold, Roger and Rupesh find themselves descending into a downward spiral of negative emotions. They wrestle with feelings of inadequacy and unworthiness, plagued by the fear that they will never be able to make amends for the pain they have caused.

Despite their efforts to suppress their guilt and justify their actions, Roger and Rupesh are unable to escape the overwhelming weight of their conscience. They come to realize that the true cost of their dishonesty is not just the damage it has caused to their relationships, but the erosion of their sense of integrity and self-respect. As they confront the harsh reality of their choices, Roger and Rupesh are forced to reckon with the consequences of their actions. They understand that to find redemption and restore their sense of self-worth, they must confront the truth head-on and take responsibility for the hurt they have caused. Only then can they begin the long and arduous journey toward healing and forgiveness.

As the web of deceit woven by Roger and Rupesh begins to unravel, they find themselves facing the harsh consequences of their actions. The people closest to them, including friends and family, struggle to trust them, unsure if they can ever truly believe anything they say. Roger and Rupesh's once-solid relationships are now strained, tainted by the shadow of their dishonesty. Feeling the weight of betrayal and isolation, Roger and Rupesh attempt to repair the damage they have caused. They reach out to their loved ones, hoping to rebuild trust and restore the bonds that have been fractured by their deception. However, their efforts are met with skepticism and doubt, as those around them struggle to forgive and forget the lies they have told.

Roger and Rupesh's journey towards redemption is fraught with challenges as they navigate the rocky terrain of rebuilding trust. They understand that repairing the damage caused by their dishonesty will not happen overnight, but they are determined to make amends and prove themselves worthy of forgiveness. Despite the obstacles they face, Roger and Rupesh remain hopeful that with time and effort, they can rebuild the trust that has been lost. They are committed to facing the consequences of their actions head-on and taking the necessary steps toward redemption, knowing that only by confronting the truth can they hope to mend the broken relationships that once meant so much to them.

Roger and Rupesh confront the harsh reality of the impact of their dishonesty on their self-image and relationships with others. They come to terms with the fact that their deceitful actions have tarnished their reputation and damaged the trust of those around them. With a heavy heart, they acknowledge that to move forward, they must confront the truth and take responsibility for their actions. Driven by a newfound sense of remorse and a desire to make amends, Roger and Rupesh embark on a journey of redemption. They reach out to those they have hurt, offering heartfelt apologies and demonstrating genuine remorse for the pain they have caused. Through acts of humility and sincerity, they strive to rebuild trust and repair the relationships that have been fractured by their dishonesty.

As they navigate the complexities of their journey, Roger and Rupesh learn valuable lessons about honesty, integrity, and the importance of owning up to their mistakes. They come to understand that true strength lies not in deception, but in the courage to face the truth and take responsibility for one's actions. Through their efforts to make amends and seek forgiveness, Roger and Rupesh begin to rebuild the trust that has been lost. They recognize that redemption is a process and that it requires patience, humility, and a willingness to confront the consequences of one's actions.

As they continue on their journey of redemption, Roger and Rupesh emerge as stronger, more resilient individuals, armed with a newfound appreciation for the power of honesty and integrity in building and maintaining meaningful relationships. They understand that while the road to redemption may be long and challenging, the rewards of living a life guided by truth and integrity are immeasurable.

CHAPTER SIX

SEEKING ANSWERS

A. Luther and Melody embark on a journey of self-reflection, seeking to understand the root causes of their son's behavior.

Luther and Melody embark on their journey of understanding by carefully observing the recurring patterns of behavior exhibited by their sons, Roger and Rupesh. They take note of the frequent requests for money and the evasive responses when questioned about their intentions. Instead of dismissing these behaviors as isolated incidents, Luther and Melody recognize them as symptoms of deeper underlying issues within their family dynamic. As they reflect on their observations, Luther and Melody begin to connect the dots between their sons' behaviors and the broader context of their family life. They consider how their actions and attitudes may have inadvertently contributed to Roger and Rupesh's tendencies to seek financial gain through deception.

With a newfound awareness of the patterns at play, Luther and Melody are determined to delve deeper into the root causes of their son's behavior. They recognize the importance of addressing these underlying issues to foster a healthier and more honest family environment. Armed with this understanding, Luther and Melody set out on a journey of self-reflection and exploration, seeking to uncover the factors that have shaped their family dynamic and contributed to their sons' deceptive tendencies. As they delve deeper into their own past experiences and parenting practices, they begin to unravel the complexities of honesty and deceit within their family, laying the groundwork for meaningful change and growth.

Luther and Melody embark on a journey of introspection, carefully examining their parenting styles and the impact they may have had on their sons' behavior. They engage in candid discussions about their approaches to discipline, communication, and setting boundaries, reflecting on whether these strategies have been effective in fostering open and honest dialogue with Roger and Rupesh. As they delve deeper into their parenting practices, Luther and Melody confront their strengths and weaknesses. They acknowledge moments when they may have been too lenient or too strict, recognizing the importance of finding a balance that encourages their sons to express themselves freely while also instilling a sense of responsibility and accountability.

With a commitment to self-improvement and growth, Luther and Melody pledge to be more mindful and intentional in their interactions with Roger and Rupesh. They seek out resources and support to help them navigate the complexities of parenting, recognizing that fostering a healthy and honest family dynamic requires ongoing effort and dedication. Through their journey of self-reflection, Luther and Melody come to understand the profound impact their parenting choices have on their sons' development. They commit to creating a nurturing and supportive environment where Roger and Rupesh feel valued and understood, laying the foundation for open communication and mutual respect within their family.

As Luther and Melody continue their journey of self-reflection, they broaden their focus to include the influence of extended family members on their sons' behavior and attitudes. They consider the role of grandparents, aunts, and uncles in shaping Roger and Rupesh's perceptions of money and honesty, recognizing that familial relationships can have a significant impact on a child's development. Luther and Melody reflect on their relationships with their parents, examining the dynamics that may be playing out in their interactions with Roger and Rupesh. They consider whether they have inadvertently inherited certain attitudes or behaviors from their upbringing, and how these may be influencing their parenting approach.

Through honest and open dialogue, Luther and Melody confront any underlying tensions or conflicts within their extended family relationships. They seek to understand how these dynamics may be contributing to their sons' behavior, and how they can work together as a family to foster a more supportive and nurturing environment for Roger and Rupesh. By acknowledging the influence of extended family members on their sons' development, Luther and Melody gain valuable insights into the broader context in which their family operates. They recognize the importance of fostering positive and healthy relationships with their relatives, while also maintaining clear boundaries and expectations for their sons' behavior. Armed with this understanding, Luther and Melody are better equipped to navigate the complexities of parenting and to create a more harmonious and supportive family environment for Roger and Rupesh to thrive.

As Luther and Melody continue their journey of introspection, they delve into the emotional needs underlying their sons' behavior. They consider factors such as insecurity, fear of failure, and the desire for validation that may be driving Roger and Rupesh's actions, recognizing that these underlying emotions play a significant role in shaping their behavior. Luther and Melody reflect on their role as parents in providing emotional support and guidance for their children. They acknowledge that while it's important to address their sons' deceptive behavior, it's equally crucial to understand the root causes behind it. By delving into their sons' emotional needs, Luther and Melody aim to create a supportive and nurturing environment where Roger and Rupesh feel understood and valued.

Through open and honest communication, Luther and Melody encourage Roger and Rupesh to express their feelings and concerns openly. They strive to create a safe space where their sons feel comfortable sharing their emotions, knowing that addressing these underlying needs is essential for fostering healthy development and behavior. Armed with a deeper understanding of their sons' emotional needs, Luther and Melody are better equipped to provide the love, support, and guidance that Roger and Rupesh need to thrive. They recognize that by addressing these underlying emotions, they can help their sons develop the resilience and confidence they need to navigate life's challenges with honesty and integrity.

As Luther and Melody come to the end of their journey of self-reflection, they emerge with a renewed sense of purpose and commitment to growth within their family. They acknowledge that understanding the root causes of their sons' behavior is just the beginning of their journey toward healing and transformation. With newfound self-awareness and a deeper understanding of their sons' needs, Luther and Melody reaffirm their dedication to fostering a supportive and nurturing environment for Roger and Rupesh. They recognize that addressing underlying emotional needs and promoting open communication are key elements in creating a healthy family dynamic built on trust and understanding.

Armed with optimism and determination, Luther and Melody embark on the journey ahead, knowing that positive change is possible through introspection and self-reflection. They embrace the challenges and opportunities that lie ahead, committed to continued growth and improvement for themselves and their children. As they move forward, Luther and Melody are guided by the lessons they have learned and the insights they have gained throughout their journey. They remain steadfast in their belief that by fostering a culture of honesty, empathy, and understanding within their family, they can create a brighter and more harmonious future for themselves and their children.

B. Conversations with Robert shed light on generational patterns of deceit and the importance of honesty in family relationships.

Luther and Melody, feeling overwhelmed by the ongoing struggles with their sons' deceitful behavior, turn to Luther's father, Robert, for guidance and wisdom. With a sense of trepidation, they approach Robert, unsure of what to expect but desperate for answers to their pressing questions. Robert welcomes their concerns with open arms and a listening ear, sensing the gravity of the situation.

He creates a safe space for Luther and Melody to express their worries and frustrations, setting the stage for deeper conversations about the importance of honesty in family relationships.

As Luther and Melody pour out their hearts to Robert, he listens attentively, offering words of comfort and reassurance. Drawing from his own experiences as a parent and grandparent, Robert shares valuable insights and wisdom, encouraging Luther and Melody to confront the underlying issues fueling their sons' deceptive behavior. Through their conversations with Robert, Luther, and Melody gain a newfound sense of clarity and perspective. They come to understand the profound impact that honesty, trust, and communication have on the fabric of their family relationships, and they are inspired to take proactive steps toward fostering a culture of openness and integrity within their home.

With Robert's guidance and support, Luther and Melody feel empowered to tackle the challenges ahead with renewed strength and determination. They are grateful for his wisdom and compassion, knowing that his guidance will continue to light their path as they navigate the complexities of parenthood and family life. Robert opens up about his own life experiences, offering Luther and Melody a window into the generational patterns of deceit within their family. With a sense of vulnerability and honesty, he shares anecdotes from his childhood and adolescence, recounting moments where dishonesty and mistrust played a significant role in shaping his relationships with his parents and siblings.

Robert's stories provide valuable insights into the complexities of family dynamics and the lasting impact of deception on familial bonds. He reveals how secrets and half-truths can erode trust and breed resentment, leaving scars that can take years to heal. Through his candid reflections, Robert helps Luther and Melody understand the deep-seated roots of their son's behavior and how it has been influenced by their family history. As Luther and Melody listen to Robert's stories, they begin to connect the dots between past and present, recognizing the echoes of their struggles within their family's narrative. They gain a deeper appreciation for the interconnectedness of their experiences and how they have been shaped by the patterns of deceit that have spanned generations.

Armed with this newfound understanding, Luther and Melody are better equipped to address the underlying issues driving their sons' behavior. They realize the importance of breaking free from the cycle of deception and fostering a culture of honesty and openness within their family. Inspired by Robert's resilience and wisdom, they are determined to chart a new course for their family—one built on trust, transparency, and mutual respect. As Luther and Melody listen intently to Robert's stories, they are struck by the poignant parallels between their own experiences and those of previous generations in their family. They come to realize that patterns of deceit and mistrust have been deeply ingrained within their family lineage, shaping their attitudes and behaviors towards honesty and integrity from a young age.

Robert's insights serve as a powerful catalyst for introspection, prompting Luther and Melody to reflect on their roles in perpetuating these destructive patterns. They begin to recognize moments in their own lives where they may have unknowingly contributed to the cycle of deceit, whether through small acts of dishonesty or by turning a blind eye to the truth. As they delve deeper into their reflections, Luther and Melody feel a sense of urgency to break free from the destructive cycles that have plagued their family for generations. They realize that to create lasting change, they must confront the past head-on and make a conscious effort to foster a culture of honesty and openness within their family.

Inspired by Robert's resilience and wisdom, Luther and Melody are determined to chart a new course for their family—one that is built on trust, transparency, and mutual respect. They recognize that breaking free from the grip of deceit will require courage and perseverance, but they are committed to taking the necessary steps to create a brighter and more authentic future for themselves and their children.

Robert challenges Luther and Melody to confront the truth about their son's behavior and the role they play in perpetuating dishonesty within their family. He encourages them to examine their actions and attitudes towards honesty, urging them to lead by example and prioritize transparency and integrity in their interactions with their children. Robert's words of wisdom serve as a catalyst for reflection and change, inspiring Luther and Melody to take proactive steps toward fostering a culture of honesty within their family. Luther and Melody feel a profound shift within themselves. Their conversations with Robert have opened their eyes to the destructive patterns that have plagued their family for generations, and they are determined to break free from the cycle of deceit once and for all.

With a renewed sense of purpose and determination, Luther and Melody commit to fostering a culture of honesty and openness within their family. They recognize the importance of honesty in building strong and resilient relationships, and they are ready to do the hard work necessary to create a healthier and more authentic family dynamic. With Robert's guidance and support, Luther and Melody embark on a journey of healing and transformation. They know that it won't be easy and that there will be challenges along the way, but they are confident that they can overcome them together.

As they lay the foundation for a brighter future, Luther and Melody are filled with hope and optimism. They are excited to see the positive impact that their newfound commitment to honesty and integrity will have on their family, and they are ready to embrace the journey ahead with open hearts and open minds.

BREAKING THE CYCLE

A. Luther and Melody confront Roger and Rupesh, encouraging open communication and accountability.

With a heavy heart and a deep sense of determination, Luther and Melody gather their courage to confront Roger and Rupesh about their deceptive behavior. They know that this conversation will be difficult and uncomfortable, but they also understand that it's necessary to address the underlying issues and move forward as a family. As they steel themselves for the confrontation, Luther and Melody reflect on their desire to foster open communication and accountability within their family. They recognize that by confronting their sons about their deceitful actions, they are not only holding them accountable for their behavior but also creating an opportunity for healing and resolution.

Despite their apprehension, Luther and Melody draw strength from their love for Roger and Rupesh, knowing that their intentions come from a place of deep care and concern for their well-being. With this mindset, they approach the conversation with a sense of determination and purpose, ready to face whatever challenges may come their way to create a brighter future for their family. With a deep breath and steady resolve, Luther and Melody sit down with Roger and Rupesh to engage in an honest dialogue about their behavior. They create a safe and non-judgmental space for their sons to express themselves, knowing that open communication is key to resolving the issues at hand.

Luther and Melody encourage Roger and Rupesh to share their thoughts and feelings without fear of reprisal, assuring them that their voices will be heard and respected. They listen attentively as their sons speak, offering validation for their emotions and concerns while also holding them accountable for their actions. Throughout the conversation, Luther and Melody remain calm and composed, offering guidance and support as Roger and Rupesh navigate their feelings of guilt and remorse. They emphasize the importance of honesty and integrity in building strong and healthy relationships, reaffirming their commitment to fostering a culture of trust and transparency within their family.

As the dialogue unfolds, Luther and Melody's hearts swell with pride as they witness the courage and vulnerability displayed by their sons. Together, they navigate the complexities of their emotions, forging a path toward healing and reconciliation that will ultimately strengthen their family bond. As the conversation unfolds, Luther and Melody emphasize the importance of accountability and the consequences of dishonesty. They lovingly but firmly make it clear to Roger and Rupesh that their actions have consequences and that they must take responsibility for their behavior.

With a gentle yet firm tone, Luther and Melody reassure their sons that they are loved and supported unconditionally, regardless of their mistakes. They emphasize that their goal is not to punish, but rather to help Roger and Rupesh learn from their actions and grow into responsible and honest individuals. Luther and Melody outline clear expectations for their sons moving forward, setting boundaries and guidelines to help prevent future instances of deceit. They emphasize the importance of honesty and integrity in building strong relationships and stress that trust must be earned through consistent and truthful behavior.

As the conversation comes to a close, Luther and Melody wrap their sons in a warm embrace, reaffirming their unwavering love and support. They remind Roger and Rupesh that they are a family and that together, they can overcome any challenge that comes their way. Luther and Melody focus on rebuilding trust with Roger and Rupesh. They express their disappointment and hurt caused by their son's behavior but also convey their belief in their ability to change and grow. Luther and Melody reaffirm their commitment to fostering a culture of honesty and integrity within their family and work together with Roger and Rupesh to repair the damage done to their relationships.

As Luther, Melody, and their sons gather together as a family, there is a sense of peace and unity in the air. They sit in a circle, holding hands, as they reflect on the progress they've made in their journey towards open communication and accountability. Luther and Melody express their gratitude for the courage and vulnerability that Roger and Rupesh have shown throughout this process. They acknowledge that the road ahead may still be challenging, but they are confident that as a family, they can overcome any obstacle that comes their way.

Roger and Rupesh, in turn, express their appreciation for their parents' unwavering love and support. They recognize the importance of honesty and integrity in building strong relationships, and they are committed to continuing to work toward positive change. As they sit together in the warmth of their love and support, Luther and Melody reaffirm their pride in their sons and their dedication to each other as a family. They know that their journey towards open communication and accountability may have its ups and downs, but they are confident that with love and support, they can overcome anything that comes their way.

B. Together, they work to foster a culture of honesty and integrity within their family.

Luther and Melody gather Roger and Rupesh together for an important family meeting, where they openly express their shared desire to cultivate a family environment grounded in honesty and integrity. They sit down together, creating a safe and welcoming space for open dialogue. Luther and Melody start by expressing their commitment to fostering a culture of trust and transparency within the family. They emphasize the importance of mutual respect and accountability, highlighting how honesty is the foundation upon which strong relationships are built.

Roger and Rupesh listen attentively as their parents speak, nodding in agreement as they recognize the value of open communication in their family dynamic. Together, they brainstorm ways to create an atmosphere where honesty is valued and dishonesty is not tolerated. They discuss the importance of actively listening to one another, being honest about their feelings, and taking responsibility for their actions. They also explore the idea of setting clear expectations and boundaries, as well as establishing consequences for dishonest behavior.

As they work together to create a plan for fostering a culture of honesty and integrity within their family, Luther and Melody feel a sense of pride and optimism. They know that by working together as a team, they can create a loving and supportive environment where everyone feels valued and respected. Luther and Melody gather their sons, Roger and Rupesh, to outline clear expectations for behavior within the family. Sitting together in a circle, they establish guidelines for honest communication, emphasizing the importance of speaking truthfully and taking responsibility for one's actions.

With a gentle but firm tone, Luther and Melody stress the importance of honesty and integrity in building strong relationships. They encourage Roger and Rupesh to ask for help when needed and to communicate openly about their thoughts and feelings, reassuring them that they will always be met with understanding and support. Luther and Melody underscore that trust is built on a foundation of honesty and integrity, and they encourage their sons to uphold these values in their interactions with others. They remind Roger and Rupesh that their words and actions have consequences and that by being truthful and accountable, they can cultivate a positive and supportive family environment.

As they conclude their discussion, Luther and Melody wrap their sons in a warm embrace, reaffirming their love and support. They express their confidence in Roger and Rupesh's ability to uphold the values of honesty and integrity, knowing that together, they can create a family dynamic built on trust and respect. As the family works to foster a culture of honesty and integrity, Luther and Melody recognize the importance of leading by example. They strive to model honesty and transparency in their actions and interactions, demonstrating to Roger and Rupesh what it means to live with integrity. Luther and Melody are mindful of their words and behaviors, knowing that their actions speak louder than words when it comes to shaping their sons' values and beliefs.

Luther and Melody are committed to nurturing open communication within their family, recognizing it as essential for building strong relationships based on honesty and respect. They intentionally create opportunities for Roger and Rupesh to express themselves freely and without judgment, fostering a safe and supportive environment where their sons feel valued and heard. Whether through regular family meetings, one-on-one conversations, or shared activities, Luther and Melody make it a priority to engage in meaningful dialogue with Roger and Rupesh. They listen actively to their sons' concerns and perspectives, offering empathy and validation as they navigate the challenges of growing up.

Luther and Melody encourage Roger and Rupesh to express themselves honestly, knowing that open communication is key to building trust and understanding within the family. They reassure their sons that their thoughts and feelings are valid and deserving of respect, fostering a sense of confidence and self-expression. As they continue to prioritize open communication, Luther and Melody lay the groundwork for stronger relationships with their sons. They know that by creating a safe space for dialogue, they can cultivate a family dynamic built on trust, empathy, and mutual respect.

As the family continues to work towards fostering a culture of honesty and integrity, Luther and Melody take time to celebrate the progress they've made together. They reflect on the positive changes they've observed in their sons' behavior and attitudes, recognizing the effort and commitment it takes to build trust and communication within a family. Luther and Melody express their pride in Roger and Rupesh for their growth and development and reaffirm their dedication to nurturing a supportive and honest family environment for years to come.

CHAPTER EIGHT

THE POWER OF TRUTH

A. Roger and Rupesh gradually learn the value of honesty and the impact of their actions on others.

After a heartfelt conversation with Luther and Melody, Roger and Rupesh embark on a journey towards understanding the value of honesty. Reflecting on past incidents where their dishonesty caused harm to others, they begin to recognize the need for change. Luther and Melody guide them through a thoughtful discussion about the importance of honesty and the impact of their actions on their family and friends. As they delve into the conversation, Luther and Melody create a safe and non-judgmental space for Roger and Rupesh to explore their feelings and experiences. They encourage their sons to reflect on the consequences of their dishonesty, both for themselves and for those around them. Through gentle guidance and empathetic listening, Luther and Melody help Roger and Rupesh gain a deeper understanding of the value of honesty in fostering trust and building strong relationships.

Roger and Rupesh begin to see how their dishonesty has affected their family dynamics and relationships with others. They express remorse for their past actions and a sincere desire to make amends. With the support and encouragement of Luther and Melody, they commit to being more truthful and accountable in their words and actions moving forward. As they continue on their journey, Roger and Rupesh embrace the importance of honesty as a guiding principle in their lives. They recognize that by being truthful and transparent, they can cultivate deeper connections with their family and friends, leading to a happier and more fulfilling existence. With Luther and Melody by their side, Roger and Rupesh embark on a path toward personal growth and positive change, knowing that honesty is the foundation upon which they can build a brighter future.

Roger and Rupesh come face to face with the consequences of their past dishonesty, witnessing firsthand the hurt and disappointment their actions have caused their loved ones. As they see the pain in Luther and Melody's eyes, they are overwhelmed with feelings of remorse and guilt. Luther and Melody provide unwavering support and encouragement, guiding their sons through this difficult realization. Together, as a family, they engage in open and honest conversations about the impact of Roger and Rupesh's behavior on their relationships and family dynamics. Luther and Melody create a safe space for their sons to express their emotions and reflect on the repercussions of their actions. They encourage Roger and Rupesh to take responsibility for their behavior and acknowledge the harm they have caused.

Through these conversations, Roger and Rupesh begin to understand the importance of accountability and the power of sincere apologies. They express genuine remorse for their past dishonesty and commit to make amends. Luther and Melody offer forgiveness and understanding, reaffirming their love and support for their sons as they navigate the path toward redemption. As Roger and Rupesh confront the consequences of their actions, they gain valuable insights into the impact of honesty and integrity on their relationships. With the guidance of Luther and Melody, they learn valuable lessons about the importance of taking responsibility for their actions and the power of sincere apologies in rebuilding trust and repairing relationships. Through this process, Roger and Rupesh begin to heal and grow, emerging as more empathetic and accountable individuals ready to embrace a future grounded in honesty and integrity.

Roger and Rupesh, confronted with the consequences of their past dishonesty, witness the profound impact their actions have had on their loved ones. They see the hurt and disappointment reflected in the eyes of Luther and Melody, recognizing the pain they have caused through their deceitful behavior. Overwhelmed with remorse and guilt, Roger and Rupesh turn to their parents for guidance and support. Luther and Melody, understanding the importance of accountability, provide a safe space for Roger and Rupesh to confront their feelings and take responsibility for their actions. They encourage their sons to reflect on the harm their dishonesty has inflicted on their family and friends, fostering a sense of empathy and self-awareness. Through open and honest dialogue, Roger and Rupesh begin to acknowledge the impact of their behavior and the need for change.

As Roger and Rupesh embrace accountability, they express a sincere desire to make amends and rebuild trust with their loved ones. Luther and Melody commend their sons for their honesty and courage, recognizing the significance of taking responsibility for their actions. They offer unwavering support and encouragement, guiding Roger and Rupesh through the process of personal growth and redemption. Together, as a family, they embark on a journey towards healing and reconciliation, united by their shared commitment to honesty and integrity. Roger and Rupesh, committed to their journey of growth and redemption, embrace honesty as a guiding principle in their daily lives. They recognize the transformative power of truthfulness and strive to embody this value in their interactions with others. Luther and Melody, proud of their sons' newfound commitment to honesty, offer encouragement and support as they navigate the challenges of living with integrity.

Roger and Rupesh make a conscious effort to speak truthfully and transparently, even when faced with difficult or uncomfortable situations. They recognize that honesty requires courage and vulnerability, but they also understand the importance of building trust and fostering authentic connections with those around them. Luther and Melody, impressed by their sons' determination, provide guidance and guidance, praising their efforts and offering constructive feedback to help them navigate the complexities of honesty. Through consistent practice and self-reflection, Roger and Rupesh begin to internalize the importance of honesty as a fundamental value in their lives. They come to understand that being honest not only strengthens their relationships with others but also enhances their sense of self-worth and integrity. With

Luther and Melody's unwavering support, Roger and Rupesh continue to grow and evolve, embracing honesty as a cornerstone of their identity.

Roger and Rupesh, having embarked on a journey of self-discovery and personal growth, fully embrace the transformative power of honesty in their lives. They reflect on the challenges they've overcome and the lessons they've learned along the way, recognizing the profound impact that living with integrity has had on their relationships and overall well-being. Luther and Melody, witnessing their sons' remarkable progress, express their pride and admiration, reaffirming their unwavering support and commitment to their continued journey toward authenticity and self-realization. Together, as a family, they celebrate the newfound sense of freedom and authenticity that comes with embracing the truth, knowing that their bond has grown stronger through honesty and mutual respect.

B. Through their journey, they discover the freedom and authenticity that comes with living a life based on truth.

As Roger and Rupesh confront the burden of deceit, Luther and Melody provide unwavering support and guidance. Together, they explore the underlying reasons behind their sons' dishonest behavior, delving into the emotions and fears that may have led them down this path. Roger and Rupesh open up about their struggles, expressing their desire for change and their longing for a life free from the weight of lies. With Luther and Melody by their side, they embark on a journey of self-discovery and transformation, determined to break free from the chains of deception and embrace a future built on honesty and integrity.

As Roger and Rupesh confront their fears about being honest, Luther and Melody stand by their side, offering unwavering support and encouragement. Together, they create a safe and nurturing environment where Roger and Rupesh feel empowered to express themselves openly and authentically. Luther and Melody share their own experiences of vulnerability and self-acceptance, reassuring their sons that embracing honesty is a courageous act that will ultimately lead to greater freedom and fulfillment. With newfound courage and determination, Roger and Rupesh take the first steps towards living a life guided by authenticity and integrity.

As Roger and Rupesh continue their journey towards embracing vulnerability, they find solace in the unconditional support of Luther and Melody. Through heartfelt conversations and shared experiences, they begin to realize that vulnerability is not a sign of weakness but rather a powerful catalyst for growth and connection. Luther and Melody celebrate their sons' courage and honesty, recognizing the strength it takes to confront their fears and insecurities head-on. With each step forward, Roger and Rupesh gain a deeper understanding of themselves and the transformative power of embracing vulnerability in their lives.

Roger and Rupesh's journey towards authenticity and truth is met with a sense of liberation and empowerment. As they shed the layers of deception and embrace their genuine selves, they experience a newfound sense of freedom and self-acceptance. Luther and Melody rejoice in their sons' transformation, witnessing the joy and peace that radiates from within them. Together, they celebrate the triumph of honesty and integrity, knowing that their family is stronger and more resilient because of it.

Roger and Rupesh's embrace of authenticity marks a significant milestone in their personal growth and development. They exude confidence and self-assurance as they navigate life's challenges with honesty and transparency, unencumbered by the weight of deception. Luther and Melody beam with pride as they witness their sons' transformation, recognizing the courage and resilience it takes to live authentically in a world that often values conformity. Together, they celebrate the triumph of integrity and the deepening of their family bonds, knowing that their collective journey toward truth has strengthened their relationships and enriched their lives.

CONCLUSION

A. Reflect on the transformative journey of Luther, Melody, Roger, and Rupesh as they navigate the complexities of honesty and deceit.

As Luther and Melody confront Roger and Rupesh about their deceptive behavior, they open the door to honest communication within the family. Together, they acknowledge the patterns of deceit that have taken root and the toll it has taken on their relationships. The family confronts the discomfort of facing the truth head-on, but they also recognize the potential for growth and healing that comes with embracing honesty and authenticity. This pivotal moment marks the beginning of their journey towards a more transparent and trustworthy family dynamic.

As Luther and Melody delve into the origins of their sons' dishonesty, they confront a myriad of factors contributing to their behavior. They reflect on their parenting styles, questioning whether their approach inadvertently fostered an environment where dishonesty thrived. Meanwhile, Roger and Rupesh grapple with their own emotions, confronting fears and insecurities that have driven them to deceive their family. Through open dialogue and introspection, the family begins to untangle the complex web of influences shaping their behavior, paving the way for deeper understanding and personal transformation.

As Luther, Melody, Roger, and Rupesh navigate their journey toward honesty and integrity, they encounter various challenges that test their resolve. They confront internal struggles, grappling with feelings of doubt and temptation as they strive to break free from old habits of deceit. Additionally, they face external obstacles, such as skepticism from others and societal pressures to conform to dishonest norms. Despite these challenges, they remain steadfast in their commitment to living authentically, drawing strength from their shared values and the unwavering support of each other. Through perseverance and resilience, they continue to push forward, determined to overcome obstacles and build a life grounded in truth and integrity.

As the family continues their journey, they experience significant moments of growth and self-discovery. Luther and Melody adopt more open and effective communication strategies with Roger and Rupesh, creating an environment where trust and understanding can flourish. Through honest and respectful dialogue, they strengthen their bond as a family and deepen their connections with one another. Roger and Rupesh undergo their transformation, developing a heightened sense of self-awareness and accountability. They confront their past mistakes with courage and humility, embracing the opportunity to learn and grow from their experiences. As they let go of the burdens of deceit, they discover the freedom and authenticity that comes with living life with integrity.

Together, the family learns valuable lessons about the power of honesty and the importance of fostering trust and transparency in their relationships. Through their collective efforts, they continue to navigate the complexities of honesty and deceit, finding strength and resilience in their shared commitment to living authentically. As Luther, Melody, Roger, and Rupesh gather to celebrate their transformative journey, they are filled with a profound sense of gratitude and pride. They reflect on the challenges they have faced and the obstacles they have overcome, recognizing the strength and resilience that lies within each member of their family.

With open hearts and minds, they acknowledge the growth they have experienced individually and collectively. Luther and Melody express their admiration for Roger and Rupesh's courage and commitment to change, while Roger and Rupesh express their gratitude for their parents' unwavering support and guidance. Together, they look toward the future with optimism and hope, knowing that their journey toward honesty and authenticity has brought them closer together as a family. They reaffirm their commitment to fostering trust and transparency in their relationships, knowing that with love and understanding, they can overcome any challenge that comes their way.

B. Leave readers with a message of hope and the importance of fostering trust and transparency within families and communities.

Luther and Melody are faced with the stark realization that their family is plagued by a lack of honesty and transparency. They observe recurring instances of deceitful behavior from their sons, Roger and Rupesh, which strain the bonds of trust within their household. Recognizing the negative impact of dishonesty on their family dynamics, Luther and Melody make a conscious decision to embark on a journey of transformation. They vow to prioritize honesty and integrity, laying the groundwork for rebuilding trust and fostering stronger connections within their family.

Luther and Melody engage in introspection, acknowledging their role in perpetuating the culture of deceit within their family. They reflect on moments when they may have turned a blind eye to their sons' dishonesty or failed to address it effectively. With a newfound sense of self-awareness, Luther and Melody confront their shortcomings as parents and commit to making positive changes. They recognize that fostering honesty and integrity requires leading by example and holding themselves accountable for their actions. With humility and determination, they embark on a journey of personal growth and transformation, determined to create a more honest and authentic family dynamic.

As Roger and Rupesh confront the consequences of their deceitful actions, they are forced to confront uncomfortable truths about themselves and their behavior. They wrestle with feelings of guilt and shame as they come face to face with the harm they've caused to their family and themselves. Through moments of deep introspection and soul-searching, they begin to realize the significance of honesty and integrity in their lives and relationships. Roger and Rupesh grapple with the realization that their dishonesty has eroded trust and damaged their relationships with their loved ones. They acknowledge the pain they've caused and the importance of taking responsibility for their actions. As they reflect on their behavior, they recognize that living a life of deceit has left them feeling hollow and unfulfilled, longing for a sense of authenticity and connection.

Driven by a desire for redemption, Roger and Rupesh commit themselves to a journey of self-improvement and personal growth. They acknowledge that rebuilding trust will take time and effort, but they are willing to put in the work to repair the damage they've done. With each step forward, they strive to embody the values of honesty and integrity, knowing that true fulfillment lies in living a life aligned with their core principles. The family's journey towards embracing honesty and transparency is marked by moments of growth and unity. Luther, Melody, Roger, and Rupesh come together with a shared sense of purpose, determined to break free from the cycle of deceit that has plagued their relationships. They support and uplift one another through the challenges they face, offering encouragement and understanding along the way.

As they navigate the complexities of their newfound commitment to living authentically, the family learns to communicate openly and honestly with each other. They create a safe and nurturing environment where everyone's thoughts and feelings are valued, fostering trust and understanding within their relationships. Through their collective efforts, they begin to mend the fractures in their family dynamic, building a stronger and more resilient bond based on mutual respect and honesty.

Together, Luther, Melody, Roger, and Rupesh embrace the possibility of change and transformation, knowing that their journey toward authenticity will be challenging but ultimately rewarding. They celebrate each other's successes and support each other through setbacks, knowing that they are stronger together than they are apart. With unwavering determination and a shared commitment to growth, the family embarks on a new chapter filled with hope, love, and the promise of a brighter future.

The family gathers together to reflect on their transformative journey and the profound growth they have experienced as individuals and as a unit. They marvel at the newfound trust and openness that has flourished within their family, realizing that honesty is the cornerstone upon which their relationships are built. Each member expresses gratitude for the opportunity to learn and grow together, acknowledging the challenges they have overcome and the resilience they have demonstrated along the way.

With renewed optimism and determination, the family extends their commitment to fostering trust and transparency beyond their household walls. They recognize the importance of spreading a message of hope and possibility to their broader community, inspiring others to embrace authenticity and integrity in their own lives. Through their example, they seek to create ripple effects of positive change, empowering others to cultivate relationships grounded in mutual respect and understanding.

As they look towards the future, the family is filled with a sense of purpose and possibility. They know that their journey toward honesty and openness is ongoing, but they are confident in their ability to navigate whatever challenges may arise together. With love, support, and a shared commitment to growth, they are ready to continue forging a path toward a brighter, more authentic future for themselves and those around them.

Epilogue

Epilogue: A Message of Hope

As the story concludes, the narrator leaves readers with a powerful message of hope and resilience. They emphasize the importance of fostering trust and transparency within families and communities, highlighting the transformative power of honesty in building strong, resilient bonds. Through their journey, Luther, Melody, Roger, and Rupesh have learned that even in the face of adversity, honesty and authenticity have the power to heal wounds, mend relationships, and create a brighter tomorrow for all.